RACING HEARTS

RACING HEARTS

Melinda Di Lorenzo

orca soundings

ORCA BOOK PUBLISHERS

Published in Canada and the United States in 2023 by Orca Book Publishers.
orcabook.com

Library and Archives Canada Cataloguing in Publication
Title: Racing hearts / Melinda Anne Di Lorenzo.
Names: Di Lorenzo, Melinda, 1977- author.
Series: Orca soundings.
Description: Series statement: Orca soundings
Identifiers: Canadiana (print) 20220472793 | Canadiana (ebook) 20220472815 |
ISBN 9781459836808 (softcover) | ISBN 9781459825277 (PDF) |
ISBN 9781459825284 (EPUB)
Classification: LCC PS8607.I23 R33 2023 | DDC jC813/.6—dc23

Library of Congress Control Number: 2022950243

Summary: In this high-interest accessible novel for teen readers, Sienna trains for a triathlon in honor of her dead best friend, while falling for a mysterious jock.

Orca Book Publishers is committed to reducing the consumption of nonrenewable resources in the production of our books. We make every effort to use materials that support a sustainable future.

Orca Book Publishers gratefully acknowledges the support for its publishing programs provided by the following agencies: the Government of Canada, the Canada Council for the Arts and the Province of British Columbia through the BC Arts Council and the Book Publishing Tax Credit.

Design by Ella Collier
Edited by Doeun Rivendell
Cover photography by Stocksy.com/Jennifer Brister

Printed and bound in Canada.

26 25 24 23 • 1 2 3 4

Chapter One

I'm Sienna Shoring, the girl with the dead best friend.

And right now I'm standing in the cafeteria at school. I'd rather be anywhere else, but I forgot my lunch. And I'd prefer to starve, but it's not an option. Starving would make my stomach growl. And no one likes a fat girl with a growling stomach.

So. Here I am. Stuck in this line, waiting to pay. My head is down. My eyes are on my tray. I'm doing my best not to look around. I don't want to know if anyone is watching me. I don't want to know if anyone is *not* watching me. That would be worse. The other kids pretending like they can't see me. Like they don't know who I am or what happened five months ago.

Because five months ago is when Stacey died.

No, says a voice in my head. *That's not quite right, is it?*

Five months ago is when Stacey killed herself. She ate a whole bottle of her uncle's sleeping pills. Then she drank most of a bottle of rum. Maybe she left behind the pain she always talked about when she was alive. But she left me behind too.

If I sound like I'm pissed off, it's because I am. I'm mad. I'm sad. I don't sleep. My stomach hurts, and I feel guilty 100 percent of the time. Stacey's gone. And I don't know how to get over it.

The only reason I'm at school now is because my dad thinks it will help. He's wrong. But summer ended, and he doesn't want me to lie in my bed anymore. It scares him. And I can't explain myself to him. Not in a way he would get.

So here I am. Standing. Waiting. Not looking. I don't need any more help being a freak. But trying so hard not to be seen…that's what lets it happen. The tater tot.

I don't see the greasy, golden nugget flying at me. It's not until it taps my ear that I know it's coming. Then it's too late. It bounces down to my chest, then from my chest to my salad. It makes a noise when it hits. *Plop-plop*. And my first reaction is to blink at it. I even think I might be seeing things. But no. The tater tot stays put.

Honestly, it's the kind of thing that used to happen all the time. Before. When Stacey was alive. And five months ago I would have ignored the whole thing. Or thrown the stupid food back.

But ever since school started again—a week ago now—not one person has picked on me. No one has really *looked* at me.

I guess when your best and only friend dies, you get a free pass. The kids who picked on you for the last eleven years suddenly...*don't*. And that's a good thing. Sort of. Except for the part where your world is a mess, and you can't even count on the jerks to continue to be jerky.

So the tater tot feels out of place. But at the same time, it's kind of like coming home after a long trip.

I have a big urge to yell, *Thank you!*

I bite my lip to keep it in. I lift my gaze, then do a slow spin as I search for the tot thrower.

The caf is silent. Sure, everyone is either staring at me or pretending not to. But there's no sign of who actually made the toss. No one is claiming it.

Who did it? I wonder. *Who had the balls to throw food at the girl with the dead best friend?*

Lots of kids have the tot boxes on their trays. Some are full, some empty. Most are in between. There's no way to know who sent the tot bomb.

Giving up, I start to spin away again. I don't make it all the way, though, before a shuffle stops me.

I pause. I narrow my eyes. And this time I see him.

Alec Quincy.

Alec is a jock, but not in the usual way.

He isn't big. Maybe five and a half feet tall, and that's with his shoes on. I'm taller by three inches. And I outweigh him by at least fifty pounds. Not that I want to admit that part out loud. But somehow he's still that guy. Head of all things sporty, king of all things nasty. Smart in a way that's mean.

A few years ago Stacey and I gave him a nickname. *Worst Nightmare.* It was one of our secrets. Something we could whisper and giggle about. Except staring at him now, it seems silly. More than silly. A waste of our time.

Oh, I still hate him. But I feel a bit sorry for him too. I remember right then that he missed the end of school last year. Super-extended vacation or something. He clearly has no clue that I'm off limits. He's just a bully who can't even bully in the right way.

Now he's standing with some other guys, a little smile on his face. He's watching me. Waiting for me to react.

I stare back at him some more, trying to decide what to do. If I should even bother. Then his mouth forms a silent word. One I recognize right away.

Fatty.

So, yeah. Okay. Maybe his smartness has a limit.

After a second, someone in his group leans over to Alec and whispers something. I don't have to hear it to be sure that it's a heads-up.

Didn't you get the memo while you were away, Alec? You didn't see it online? Stacey OD'ed. We gotta leave Sienna alone.

Alec's eyes widen a bit, and I wish it made me feel better. Instead I'm just sadder. For him. For me. For Stacey. For the general upset in the school kingdom.

I can't take it anymore. Not at this moment.

Balancing my tray on one hand, I lift the other to get the tater tot. It's going to meet a fate in the trash. But then something else happens. It's weirder than all the other stuff, past or present. Someone *else's* fingers land in my salad. They take hold of the deep-fried piece of potato. They toss it into the air in an arc. It sails up. It drops down. It lands straight into a waiting mouth. And it's a mouth I know. Because it's a mouth every straight girl in a five-mile radius knows.

Chapter Two

Blake goddamn Romano.

He's six feet of perfection. And yeah. That perfection includes his curved, soft-looking lips and his straight, brace-free teeth.

A hundred times, I've wished I could be immune to his mouth. To all of him, actually. Really, his mouth is just one of my worries. There's also his dark hair with its nice wave. His wide shoulders and strong arms. His perfect skin. The way he dresses— nice but not douchey. And there are his eyes, which are the color of chocolate. I hate myself for even thinking that last thing.

The color of chocolate? Jesus, Sienna. Get a grip.

It's true, though. They *are* the color of chocolate. And I'm for sure not immune to that either.

It'd be a lie to say I haven't thought about what it would be like to kiss him. Or even talk to him, for that matter. Once I heard him laughing in the hallway, and I stopped to wish he was laughing with me.

Yeah, okay. But have you ever thought about him stealing a tater tot from your lunch tray?

The answer to that is a big, giant no. Obviously. Because I haven't moved since he did it. In fact, I'm still standing there. Watching as Blake chews up the tater tot, then tips a smile my way. And of *course* he doesn't have any food stuck in his teeth after.

"Hey, Sienna," he says.

My heart does a little flip at the fact that he knows my name. I admit it. Even though it's silly to think he wouldn't know it. Our school isn't that big. And Blake was in my math class last year. He sat right behind me for an entire month. He got an A. I remember he was super happy about the grade. And now that I'm thinking about that stuff, it would be weirder for him *not* to know my name. So maybe it's not the knowing part of it. Maybe it's just him saying it that's making my skin tingle. Or maybe—

Chill the hell out, Sienna, I tell myself. *Stop standing here like a goof. Answer him.*

"Hey," I manage to say.

My voice is a squeak. But Blake either doesn't notice or doesn't care.

"How's the salad?" he asks.

"Um," I reply. "I haven't had a bite yet."

"Oh. Yeah. I guess not. Can't eat our salad before we pay for it." He flashes another smile. "But just in case you were wondering...the potato things are good."

"Okay."

"Don't tell the lunch lady that I said so. Don't wanna ruin my rep."

"Okay," I repeat.

I shift from one foot to the other, not sure what else to say. He's close enough that his scent slides up my nose. I know what the smell is called. *Sandalwood.* I found that out by chance, sniffing the candles in a bookstore. I bought one, and I burned it in my room. Stacey teased me, calling it my "stinky dude candle." But I never did tell her it wasn't just any dude. It was Blake. The way he smelled all year in math class. Admitting my crush would've been way beyond embarrassing. So I kept it a secret.

But I'd love to tell her about it now, I think.

A little squeeze tries to take over my gut. It's the grief. The counselor says it might never go away.

Even if it does get weaker. Apparently, once I've grown up, it will still come. I'll see or hear or think of something that makes me remember Stacey. And bang. The sadness will hit, and it'll feel just like this. A tightness in my stomach and a burn in my throat.

I start the little count to ten that I've learned in my sessions, but I only make it to three. Then Blake steps closer and kind of reaches around me. His chest presses to my chest. One of his arms comes up over my shoulder too. I have no clue what he's doing. But do I care? Not really. I can smell extra sandalwood. And he's warm. Being this close to him feels good enough to make me dizzy.

The caf and the kids around me go blurry. It's not like they don't exist. But it's like they don't matter.

The weird, hug-like pose seems to last a million years. But at the same time it's over too quickly. It ends when Blake leans away and drops a fresh container of tater tots onto my tray.

"There," he says. "Replaced the one I ate. With an upgrade. And don't worry. I'm buying."

My eyes drop to the food, then come back up to his face. My cheeks are burning. Does he think that I'm too fat to *just* be eating the salad? Is he making fun of me? Not that he's gone out of his way to be a jerk in the past. But it would make a lot more sense than all this niceness. He's on the soccer team and the basketball team. Same as Alec.

"You okay?" Blake asks.

His face is crinkled up in what looks like real concern.

"I wasn't having any tater tots," I blurt.

"Yeah," he replies. "I know."

"So you don't need to buy me any," I say.

He shows me his perfect teeth, bends forward and whispers, "It's in case you want to fire back at that asshole, Alec."

Then he *winks*. It should've been cheesy, but instead my heart does another flip. Blake Romano just winked at me. And now he's grabbing another tater tot from my tray. He tosses it up and catches it just like the last one.

"See you later, Sienna," he says.

He turns and walks away, pausing to drop five bucks at the caf's till. I want to look back toward Alec and the rest of the crowd. My mind spins with questions. Were they watching this weirdness? Are they still watching it? What do they think? Do they hate that Blake spoke to me? What do *I* think? Was he being nice because of Stacey?

Why the hell does it even matter?

Then a crackling voice comes on the overhead speakers, and I forget all about Alec and Blake and the tater tot.

"Sienna Shoring to the office, please," says the voice. "That's Sienna Shoring to the office."

I shiver. Because the last time I was called down,

I found my dad standing there with bad news written all over his face. That was the day I became the girl with the dead best friend.

Chapter Three

By the time I reach the office, my legs are wobbly with nerves. A little voice in my head reminds me that the worst thing has already happened. I've already lost Stacey. But there's another voice that insists something else can always go wrong. And the second voice is louder.

It's when you let your guard down, it says. *That's when it happens.*

My shoulders are so stiff that they hurt as I push open the door and step into the office.

I stall partway in. My feet are too heavy, and I stare at them. They're heavier than the bricks my dad used to build our backyard firepit. My head feels the same way. Or worse. It doesn't want to lift up. I make myself do it anyway.

I let out a breath and think, *Thank God.*

No blue-uniformed officers are standing in front of the desk this time. Neither is my dad. It's only Ms. Inkling, the office assistant. Everyone hates her. They make fun of her crooked teeth and her old-lady perm. But I've never been happier to see someone.

"Sienna!" she says, smiling a second too late to be real. "How *are* you?"

I want to ask her how she *thinks* I am. Does she want to know about the tater tot? About my shitty sleep last night too?

I also want to point out that she's never asked me about my feelings before Stacey died. Not once.

Not even the time I came to the office with a split lip. Not the time I got my period in French class and had to beg to be let out early without permission.

But I don't say any of that stuff. I just give her the answer I know she's hoping to hear.

"I'm okay," I say.

"Good, good." She sounds relieved. "Glad to hear that."

"Thanks."

"I'm doing fine too."

I shift on the spot and clear my throat. "Someone, uh, called me to the office?"

"Right. That was me. A package for you came here to the school," she says.

My nerves come back. "It did?"

Ms. Inkling nods. "It did. And we wouldn't normally—well. Never mind. It doesn't matter, does it?" She grabs a shimmery silver envelope from the desk and holds it out to me. "Here you go, Sienna."

"Thank you."

I start to lift my hand to take the envelope from her, but the names on it catch my eye. And I freeze. Not just on the outside, but on the inside too.

Sienna Shoring and Stacey Blackmore. Care of: Tildemort Bay High School.

The rest of the words blur together as a wave of dizziness hits me. Ms. Inkling says my name. I hear her like I'm underwater. I would answer her, except I can't move.

This is what it feels like to get a message from a ghost, I think.

A shiver takes me by surprise. My head spins. Ms. Inkling says my name again, and now she sounds worried.

On the subject of names, did she notice Stacey's there beside mine?

I still can't make my lips work.

Why would Stacey send something to me—to us— at the school? Because she *must* have sent it. Who else would put both our names on something?

A dark thought hits me. It's *so* dark, and it hits me *so* hard, that my breath catches. What if she sent it here because she knew she'd be gone already when it came? What if she sent it to the school to make sure I wasn't all alone when I got it?

"Sienna?" says Ms. Inkling. "I'm going to call the nurse."

I finally manage to gasp something out. "No!"

"Are you sure?" she asks. "You're a bit pale."

I exhale and nod, then force my hand up to take the package. It's slippery in my grip. I have to tighten my fingers to keep from dropping it.

"Thank you," I say.

I leave the office fast. But once I'm in the hallway, I slow down. Do I even want to know what's inside the envelope?

The bell rings, and I jump.

"What do I do?" I whisper to myself.

It's Stacey's voice that answers in my head. *Go to math class. Duh.*

I listen to her. Mostly because there's no other choice. I've missed too much school already. But the package stays on my mind.

What should I do with it?

I hear barely anything the math teacher says. The class goes on forever. And history, my last subject of the day, is even worse. My knee won't stop bouncing. My brain buzzes.

Do I want to tear open the envelope? Or do I want to throw it away?

I'm glad that no one calls on me for an answer.

I think about my best friend too.

Seriously, Stacey. Why did you do this?

My heart starts to hurt again, and I do my best to focus. I fail. My eyes stick to the clock instead of the schoolwork.

By the time the final bell goes, I'm a weird combo of excited and scared. I rush to my locker and open it with shaking hands. My palms are so sweaty that I drop the envelope twice. The first time, I grab it. But the second time, it skids across the floor and stops three feet away.

Groaning, I bend over and reach for it. But before my fingers get to the envelope, they hit the tip of a big black boot.

Automatically my shoulders roll inward. It's a self-defense thing. An attempt to be smaller. Less noticeable. *Thank you, years of torment.*

I remind myself that no one is picking on me now. I mean, no one except for Alec and his tater tot. And he's never worn anything but running shoes in his life. The boots by my hand aren't his. I have no reason not to lift my head and meet the person's eyes. But before I straighten up, I take a breath. Right away sandalwood fills my nose. It's just enough of a warning. Blake Romano has joined me. Again.

"Hey, Sienna," he says for the second time today.

Can things get any weirder at all?

I don't think so. But then they do.

Chapter Four

"Can I walk you home?" Blake asks.

The question catches me by surprise. My lips refuse to unlock so I can answer him. I rock back on my heels, all kinds of awkward.

He has the envelope in his hands, and my face gets hot. I want to grab the shiny package and hide it behind my back. Maybe run away while I'm at it.

Instead I just stand there. It's Blake who speaks again.

"This is a Try-It Triathlon shirt, isn't it?" he asks, holding out my envelope.

I blink and take it from him. "Uh."

What the hell, Sienna? Have you forgotten about words?

But I can't talk. Because I just realized he's right.

Fucking hell, Stacey, I think.

Last spring she signed us up for the triathlon. As a joke. But it's not funny right now.

As I stare at Blake, I brace for a comment about my weight. Or for a look up and down at my non-athletic body. He doesn't do either thing. He nods.

"It's a pretty rad race," he says. "I did it last year."

Of *course* he's done it before. And of *course* he thinks it was awesome.

Answer him, I tell myself.

"Yeah," I say, clearing my throat. "We were planning on it."

The "we" slips out. So does the "were."

What the hell is wrong with me today? None of this is Blake's business. *I'm* not Blake's business.

I wait for a comment about Stacey. Something that doesn't mean a damn thing. But Blake surprises me again. I'm losing track of just how many times he's done it so far.

"I think you should do the race," he says. "But you want some advice?"

"Sure?" My reply sounds like a question, and I know it.

"If you decide to do the triathlon, make sure you train for it," he says.

Here it comes, I think. *You need to train because no way are those extra pounds helping you out.*

Blake runs his hand over his hair, and the motion doesn't even mess up the perfection. "Set aside a time to run. And to bike and swim. Get up at six in the morning and do it then, if that's when you have time."

That's it?

"Um. Okay. Thanks." I toss on my backpack and tighten the straps. "Tip noted."

I turn away. But the moment I move, Blake follows.

Is he serious right now? He wants to walk me home for real?

I steal a glance his way as he keeps pace with me. His hands are in the pockets of his baggy jeans, and his bag is hanging on one shoulder. His black shirt is the exact perfect amount of faded. His dark hair flops just like it's supposed to.

Dammit.

He looks...right. Comfortable. Like an ad for some clothing store. He even greets a few people with a slick nod. He laughs when some dude gives him a punch in the arm. But if he notices that I'm invisible, he doesn't say.

The whole thing might've pissed me off. How can he possibly not notice the difference between us?

Between the way people *treat* us? But I feel like it isn't quite real. It gets a little worse, too, as we make our way outside.

Blake opens the door. Then he holds it for me, like some polite old man. And I step through it. Like it's something I'm supposed to do. But when it comes down to it, being hit with a tater tot was more normal.

But here we are.

We walk through the schoolyard, then cross the road. We step around one street corner, and then a second. Blake is quiet. I'm quiet. Finally I can't stand it anymore.

"Is this some kind of joke?" I ask.

Blake stops so fast that it takes me a second to notice. I walk past him. But when I realize, I don't move closer. I spin around, stand still and wait.

"A joke about what?" he asks.

I swing an arm over the space between us. My bracelets jingle.

"This," I say.

His perfect eyebrows crowd together in a frown. "Your jewelry?"

"What?" I say. "No. *You.*"

"Me?" he replies.

"Yes!" I almost yell. "Eating my tater tot. Helping me pick up my stuff and holding the door. Walking me home."

"For starters," he says, "you told me you *weren't* eating the potato puff. And helping someone pick something up is, like, basic human decency. Holding doors is polite, and my grandma would freak if I didn't do it. And walking you home…" He shrugs. "Thought you might need a bodyguard."

I open my mouth, then close it. I don't know what to say. And I don't think it's fair that he keeps throwing me off.

Guys like Blake should be predictable. They're supposed to ignore me, like everyone else. And if he thinks I need a bodyguard, he must know at least a little about me. Enough to also know that his "basic human decency" claim doesn't apply. Not where his buddies are concerned anyway.

"Okay, look," I say. "I'll give you the tater tot thing. But that's it. I call bullshit on the rest of your speech."

I spin away, and this time the weirdest thing yet happens. Blake's fingers close on my elbow. And they're warm. Very warm. And nice, even though his palm is rougher than I would've expected. If I *had* an expectation, of course. Which I didn't.

More abruptly than I mean to, I shake off his grasp and step away.

He lifts both his hands in a surrendering gesture.

"I'm sorry," he says. "I didn't mean to—could you just—sorry."

The reddish tone under his olive skin makes me pause. He looks uncomfortable. Embarrassed. Having every eye in the cafeteria fixed on him had less effect.

He clears his throat. "I didn't mean to grab you. Swear to god. But could you give me another second? Or, like, sixty of them?"

"It's fine," I lie. "Just give me some warning next time you're going to manhandle me."

The side of his mouth twitches like he's trying not to smile. I fight a groan as I clue in. I said "next time," hinting that it could happen again. From someone else, it might've seemed like flirting. My face warms, and I cross my arms over my chest.

"Your sixty seconds are ticking," I state.

Blake does the hand-over-hair thing again. "I saw Alec throw the food. And it was shitty."

"Well, *I* know that," I reply. "But I've known it for ten years or so."

"Right," he mutters. "Gonna have to do better."

Damn right you are, I think.

"Can we walk?" he asks after a long pause.

I shrug. "Sure. Why the hell not?"

We start moving again, and I get the feeling he's trying to work up the nerve to say something. It's so ironic that I want to laugh.

Blake Romano. Last year the other students voted him Most Likely to Become a Male Model. It says so in the yearbook. And he's nervous about talking to *me*. Sienna Shoring. Last year my biggest claim to fame was the time I slipped on a pencil and knocked out a front tooth. Or it *was* before Stacey died.

Blake is still quiet, and I wonder if I should dismiss my belief that he wanted to walk *and* talk. But at last he speaks up.

"She was in my creative writing class," he says.

And he doesn't have to tell me who he means. I know it's Stacey.

Chapter Five

For what feels like the millionth time, I don't know what to say.

I sure as hell can't tell Blake that I know he shared a class with my best friend. I'm not going to admit that she told me about some of his stories. Or that he might be good at writing.

I give my best casual shrug. "She might've mentioned it. I'm not sure."

"We talked sometimes," he says.

Well, that's news. Of all the things Stacey ever said about Blake, talking to him wasn't one of them. Panic tickles at me.

Shit. What did they talk about? Oh God. Did she talk about me?

I wait for Blake to add something else. My nerves dance and dance in my stomach. But for a long time, he says nothing. The only sound is the matching tap of our feet hitting the ground, side by side.

After a gazillion minutes of quiet, Blake sighs. But when he speaks again, his words have nothing to do with Stacey or creative writing.

"I saw Alec throw the tater tot," he states.

"Yeah," I reply, puzzled. "You told me."

"The guy's a jerk," he says.

"You think?" It's impossible to keep the sarcasm out of my voice.

He stuffs his hands into his pockets. "I'm sorry."

What is Blake even apologizing for? For Alec being a total ass? It isn't like it's Blake's fault. And if he thinks it *is* his fault, then his sorry is about ten years too late.

At least my brain and my mouth manage to work together to answer him with something smartish.

"I forgive you," I say.

He laughs. And I can't lie. I like the way it sounds. It's one of those laughs that makes your skin tingle. For a second I even relax enough that my shoulders don't pinch so much. Maybe I smile a bit too. But it doesn't last. Only until Blake slows down and points.

"Is that your house?" he asks.

I follow the direction of Blake's finger. He's right. We've almost reached my place. It's hard to miss. The blue paint is brighter than any other on the block, because my dad's a painter.

How does Blake know where I live?

I have no clue. I can't even guess. No one from school other than Stacey has been here since third grade.

We slow down even more, and a thought occurs to me. And even though it's a silly one, it sticks in my head.

Maybe in five minutes, I'll wake up and realize I was dreaming.

It's not like any of this feels real.

I have an urge to say or do something wild. To scream at the top of my lungs. To grab Blake's hands and drag him into a dance. At least it would help me figure out whether I'm awake.

Because dream-me wouldn't let my neighbors freak out and call the police. She wouldn't let dream-Blake be grossed out either. Dream-him would grab me and pull me close. Like the hero in a romance movie. He'd press his soft-looking lips to mine in the world's best first kiss ever.

But if I am awake...

I'll drop dead of embarrassment. Or worse, I won't die. And I'll be stuck with having thrown myself at Blake. Not a risk I'm willing to take. So I settle for an old-fashioned method—giving the inside of my arm a sharp pinch. It stings and makes me cringe. Definitely awake. Which is a good hint to cut the day off before it warps into something even weirder.

We come to a stop in front of my wooden gate, and Blake looks at me like he's waiting for something.

"I guess your mission was successful," I say.

"My mission?" he replies.

"To, uh...guard my body. From tater tots. Or whatever." I want to clap my hand over my mouth.

Seriously, Sienna? Did you say that out loud?

But Blake laughs, then grins one of his perfect, even-toothed grins. I work at not liking it too much.

"So..." I say. "See you around."

His smile stays. "See you, Sienna."

I grab the gate and push it open. I make sure not to look back. But halfway up the stone path, Blake's voice stops me.

"Wait!" he calls.

I turn around. His hands are in his pockets again, stuffed even farther in than earlier. He's got that awkward look now too. The one that doesn't suit him at all.

So, so much irony, I think.

"Did I forget something?" I ask.

He shakes his head. "No, but I was wondering… have you ever been to Lively Lake?"

The question catches me off guard. Not that I knew *what* to expect. Again. But not something so random.

"It's the swimming hole out behind the farmlands," Blake adds.

"No." I pause. "I mean, yes." My face is heating up, and I take a breath and try again. "Yes, I know where it is." I don't mention that it's the last place I saw Stacey. "Why are you wondering?"

"It's a good place for a run," he says.

"Oh."

He looks at me like I should say something else about the lake. But my mind rolls backward to a conversation with Stacey. One where she told me about a story Blake had written for creative writing. It took place at a lake. It involved a boy and a girl and a car. From what Stacey said, the teacher had shut the class down just when it got interesting.

I think it was about to become porn, she'd told me.

I'd thought she was lying. I'd forgotten about it. Until now. Which is—of course—the worst timing in the world. My face is no longer just warm. It's burning. Like I have a fever. I have to get out of here.

"Thanks for the tip," I say quickly. "If I'm going to run, I'll check it out."

"Don't forget about 6:00 a.m.," he reminds me.

I nod. "Right. I won't."

This time I manage to make it to my front door. It takes me two tries to get the lock open. Once I step inside, I open my backpack right away. I swear I'm going to yank out the shiny triathlon package and toss it into the garbage. But for some reason…I don't. Instead I pull my phone from my bag and set my alarm for five thirty in the morning.

Chapter Six

If I said my first attempt at a morning run went well, I'd be lying.

My alarm *does* go off the next day. It *does* wake me up. But I smack my phone so hard that I have to check if it's broken. And I go back to sleep.

The second day is the same. And the third. Alarm. Awake. Phone smack. Sleep.

I almost hope to see Blake. Maybe he has some more tips. But I have no classes with him, and I'm not going near the caf and the tater tots. And I'd rather die than set foot in the school gym. I don't want to run the triathlon *that* badly. I don't want to run it at all.

But for some reason, I keep trying. On the third night, I turn to the trusty old internet for help. And I take all its advice.

I lay out my clothes before bed.

I set a backup alarm, *and* I put my phone across the room so I can't smash it.

I put my shoes by the door.

I go to bed confident. And it works. Fourth time is the charm, I guess. At two minutes past six, I step into the cool air. My earphones are in, and my runners are laced up. But I make it only as far as the sidewalk before I have to stop. Not because my planning has fallen through. But because Blake is standing there in a hoodie and sweatpants, blocking my way.

"Morning," he says.

How does he make that sound normal?

"Uh," I reply. "Hi?"

"Jogging?" he asks.

I frown. "Yeah, but how did you know I'd be out here today but not the other days?"

"I didn't," he says. "I came those mornings too."

I'm glad the cold has probably already made my cheeks pink. "Oh."

"So…" He gestures to the sidewalk.

I blink. "You're running with me?"

"Hoping to." He shrugs. "If that's okay."

No, I think. *It's not okay. Not at all.*

Out loud, I say, "Yeah, it's, uh…that's fine."

Hoping not to talk, I turn to take off. But Blake's hand comes up to my elbow, just like it did a few days earlier. And also just like a few days earlier, him touching me is nice.

"You can't go," he tells me. "You have to warm up."

"Right."

I know that, obviously. But I'm jumpy. And worse than that, when Blake's hand drops away, I wish it hadn't. I cover up my disappointment by starting to walk.

"Did you make a route?" he asks.

"Half a mile to start." It sounds short, so I quickly add, "Plus warmup and cooldown. But I guess that'll be easy for you compared to Lively Lake or whatever."

"Actually, I hate running," he says.

"But aren't you..." I trail off and shrug.

He flashes a grin. "On the basketball, baseball and football teams?"

"Yes."

"And soccer. I am. Or was, I mean. Not anymore." His smile falls away, and he runs his fingers through his hair. "C'mon. Let's go."

He stuffs his earbuds in, so I turn on my music too. Our walk becomes a light jog.

At first it feels weird. Not just because I'm running. That's weird enough. But having someone beside me doubles the oddness. Having *Blake* beside me triples it.

Soon my lungs burn, and my legs hate me. But after a few minutes, I get into a rhythm. I even shrug off my jacket and tie it around my waist. And the music in my ears distracts me from my embarrassment.

We keep going until my phone beeps with a notification that we've hit my goal. I'm breathless. In pain. But I'm also super impressed with myself. I feel brave enough to pull out my earphones and ask a question as we start our cooldown.

"Why...aren't...you...sport...ing?" I gasp.

Blake laughs, and his breathing is fine as he replies, "Sporting?"

I wave my hand. "You...know...what...I mean."

"It didn't suit me anymore," he says.

"Sounds like…an excuse," I tell him.

"It's the truth."

"But *why*?"

"Why are you running the triathlon?" he asks.

I've almost caught my breath now, and my next words come out nearly normal. "You can't…answer a question…with a question."

"I think I just did," he says. "You show me yours, and I'll show you mine."

"Aren't we a little old to be playing doctor?"

Blake laughs, and I have to admit I like that it's because of my bad joke. I'm glad I made it.

"I hope I never get *that* old." He gives me a look that makes my skin tingle, then nudges my shoulder with his own. "Tell me."

I turn my eyes forward and do my best to explain without sounding like a complete geek. Stacey and I were standing in front of the poster that advertised the triathlon. A group of guys walked by. One made fun of the size of my butt. They called us both a couple of try-hards. But Stacey laughed in their faces. She pointed to the poster and said maybe we were going to *try hard* at the triathlon.

"They dared us to register." My throat aches with sadness as I finish. "So we did."

"You miss her," Blake replies.

It's an obvious statement, but I nod anyway. And maybe the run loosened my brain because I start talking without meaning to.

"Every day, I wake up and forget," I say. "I have to stop and think about it. No Stacey stealing my granola bar. No Stacey sticking her stuff in my locker. No Stacey at all." I make myself stop before I blurt out even more. "Sorry."

"Don't be," Blake replies.

He nudges my shoulder again, and his knuckles brush the back of my hand. I get breathless again, and now it has nothing to do with running.

I swallow and inch away. "Okay, now it's your turn. Tell me why you quit all the sports."

But Blake stops walking and points. "Can't. You're already home."

He's right. We're in front of my house. I can see my dad in the window. He's got a coffee at his lips, and he's peering out at us. He lifts a hand in a wave. I stifle a groan, but Blake just waves back.

"Guess I should go," he says. "My dad has a thing today, and he needs me to babysit my twin sisters. Thanks for hanging out with me."

He pivots and jogs off, far faster than we were moving while on our run.

I watch him go.

Now I have even more unanswered questions. And I'm starting to wonder if Blake's doing it on purpose. And if he is...then why?

Chapter Seven

The rest of the day passes in a tired blur. Every second, my body keeps reminding me that I ran. When I go up the stairs. When I stand up from a chair. When I breathe. There isn't a muscle that doesn't scream.

This is what you get, Sienna.

I'm so sore that I decide to never exercise again. I don't even pretend to set my alarm for another jog.

But the next morning, my dad wakes me up with a knock on my door.

"What?" I call from under my pillow.

"That boy is outside," he replies. "And he's got two bikes."

I repeat myself. "What?"

"That boy—"

I cut him off and sit up straight. "Shit!"

Blake.

"Language, Sienna," my dad says.

"Sorry." I toss aside my blanket, and my body starts screaming again. "Did you tell him to go away?"

"Is that what you want me to do?" my dad asks.

I think about it. I have no intention of running. But did my dad say *bikes*? Not that I'm going to do that either. But if Blake made that much effort, then I can at least tell him to go away myself.

"No," I say. "I'll come. Just yell out the window for him to wait or something."

"Got it," my dad replies.

He disappears, and I stand up and groan. And I groan again when I catch my reflection in the mirror. But I'm too tired and sore to bother with more than the basics. Blake or no Blake. I finger-comb my hair and toss it in a bun. I splash water on my face and brush my teeth. Still in my PJs, I head downstairs. And I groan a third time. Because Blake is sitting at the table with my dad, munching on a piece of toast.

"Dude, really?" I say.

"Morning, Sienna," Blake replies.

"Morning, Sienna," my dad echoes.

"I'm going back to bed," I say.

"Blake says you're doing day two of triathlon training," my dad tells me.

"Yeah, well. Blake is full of you-know-what," I reply.

They both laugh, and I narrow my eyes. Still, somehow, I find myself coasting along behind Blake on the sidewalk a few minutes later. I have a bright pink helmet on my head and a scowl on my face. But just like with the running, I get into a rhythm. It's been years since I rode a bike. The last one I had was as pink as this helmet, and it had a flower-covered basket.

I don't know how far we ride. Pretty soon I don't even know where we are. But Blake does. He keeps leading the way until we get to a park I've never seen before. He stops there and collapses on the grass. I come to an awkward stop beside him.

"You gonna stay up there?" he asks.

"Maybe I am," I say.

But a second later I hop off and sit beside him. The grass is cool. It feels good under my exercise-warmed skin.

Blake flops back and stares up at the sky. "What do you think?"

Nervously I lie down too. "That the cloud on your left looks like a monkey riding a jet ski?"

He laughs, and the sound is close to my ear. "Not about that. About the bike ride."

"I think that if you bring me a bathing suit next, I'm going to change my address," I say.

Blake laughs again, and this time the sound is even closer. *So* close that it startles me, and I turn toward him. His face is *right there.* Inches from mine.

Bet you're glad you brushed your teeth, huh? Seeing as he's near enough to kiss.

The thought makes me blush, and I quickly turn and look up again.

"Thank you," I say. "For bringing the bike and stuff."

"Happy to." He pauses. "Your dad seems nice."

"He *is* nice," I reply. "It's kind of annoying, actually."

"My dad's a hard-ass, but he could be worse." Blake rolls to his side, and I can feel his eyes on me. "He probably expects me home soon."

Disappointment rushes in, and I shove it aside. "Babysitting again?"

"Yeah. Dad's got another thing. Sucks."

"What about your mom?"

"What about *your* mom?" he replies.

His tone is flat. Like it's something he'd rather not talk about. But I feel annoyed. It's like Blake can ask whatever he wants and expects me to answer. And he already knows things about me and Stacey and won't say what exactly. But then he just refuses to answer me anytime I ask *him* something. So I push it.

"My mom took off when I was six," I say. "Haven't seen or heard from her since."

His voice loses its flatness, and he picks at the grass between us. "My mom's gone too. Almost five years now. That's her bike you're riding."

"Sorry." I mean it.

"Don't worry. She's not using it." He drops a handful of grass on my chest.

"Hey!" I roll a little and give him a shove. "Not nice."

He grins, and his eyes land on my lips. My breath catches in my throat. For a second I swear he's going to kiss me. I hold still. Blake gets the tiniest bit closer. My eyes start to close. But at the last moment, he pulls away, leaving me with a weirdly empty feeling.

"Come on," he says. "I'll race you back."

"You've got to be kidding," I reply.

But he's already on his feet and climbing back onto his bike. I scramble to catch up.

For most of the way back, he stays a few bike lengths ahead of me. Probably a good thing, considering I still have no idea which way we're going. But right before we reach my block, Blake's tire hits a rock. His bike wobbles. He hollers something I can't hear, then brakes.

I'm breathing hard, but I take advantage. I pedal faster. My bike glides past his. I cross the road while he gets stopped by a car. And in the end, I win. Fair and goddamn square.

"What's my prize?" I ask when Blake comes skidding up beside me.

He rolls his eyes, but after a second, he says, "I stopped playing sports because I didn't have time after my mom was gone. I tried. For, like, a whole year I kept playing everything. Then I cut down to just soccer for another year. Almost two, actually. But it still stressed out my dad. My sisters were eating like shit. So I gave it all up to help out."

I'm speechless. I think my mouth even hangs open a little. How had I not noticed that he wasn't on all those teams? But then again, why *would* I notice? Just because I think he has nice lips doesn't mean I pay attention to what goes on with him and his friends. The opposite, really. I avoid them at all costs.

"Hang on to the bike," he says. "But my sister will probably want that helmet back soon."

Then he takes off, leaving me staring.

Chapter Eight

The next day is Monday, but it's a day off school.
I set my alarm anyway, just like I've been doing.
When it rings, I hop out of bed. I still hurt all over,
but I ignore it. My mind buzzes. My skin prickles.

What will Blake bring today? I wonder.

"Not a swimsuit," I say to my reflection in the
mirror. "For real."

I get changed quickly into my running stuff. And while I'm laughing about *having* running stuff, I hurry downstairs. My dad has gone to work early. I steal a few sips of coffee, take a bite of a banana and go to the window. Blake's not there.

"Dammit," I say.

Then I cringe at myself.

You were hoping that badly he'd come?

Maybe I was.

"Dammit again," I say.

For a few minutes I pace around the house. I redo my ponytail three times. I brush my teeth again too. Finally I admit he's not coming.

He didn't say he'd be here, did he?

No, he didn't.

Shoving my disappointment aside, I go for my run alone. It's not so bad. I manage to keep going for almost a whole mile. My music helps me along. Afterward I hop on the bike for a short trip too. But when I get back to the house, I check my phone and sigh. Now I'm hoping he'll call?

"Pathetic," I tell myself.

But it's super hard to let it go. When my dad gets home from work, I almost hope he'll ask me about Blake. Isn't that a thing normal dads do? Ask their daughters about the boys who hang around? Threaten to pull out the shotgun or whatever?

But my dad hasn't been "normal" since my mom left. He cares. I know he does. But I think he doesn't know what to say to me sometimes. He gave me a puberty book when I was eleven. He left it on my dresser without a word.

That night we eat pizza. Talk about some cat he saw at work. Then I do the homework I've been avoiding all weekend. And we both go to bed.

Blake is the last thing I think about before I fall asleep. And he's the first thing on my mind when I wake up on Tuesday too.

The way his lips curve.

His sandalwood scent.

How he looked when I thought he might kiss me.

My brain buzz today is ten times wilder than it was yesterday.

I make up a plan for what I'm going to say to him at school. I'm going to start with a nerdy accusation about him being abducted by aliens. He'll laugh. Then I'll tell him about my run and my ride. I'll tell him I didn't go this morning, and I'll blame him. He'll laugh again.

But none of it happens. The whole day, I don't even see Blake. Not all that unexpected. Like I said before, we don't have classes together. We clearly don't have the same friends.

But still...

I go home feeling sad. My dad even asks what's wrong. I smile and lie about getting a bad mark on a test.

Determined to prove I don't need Blake, I set my alarm and run on Wednesday morning.

I pretend not to hope I'll see him at school. Which is good. Because I don't.

On Thursday I get up and bike.

I go to school.

I eat by myself.

I coast through my classes on autopilot.

I don't make eye contact with the girls I run into in the bathroom.

Nothing is any different than it has been my whole life.

On Friday I don't run or bike. I admit that it wasn't reasonable to think one weekend with Blake would change anything. Nothing else has ever done it.

That afternoon at lunch, I get a headache. I text my dad to be excused from class and get ready to go home. It's then that I finally see Blake.

He's in the hallway, surrounded by a group of other dudes. My heart rate goes up, even though I tell it not to.

Does he see me?

I wait a little while, kind of standing by my locker. His eyes come up once. And that's it. He goes back to talking to his friends. I realize again how ridiculous it was to think that things might be different.

Stacey would've warned me. She would've made fun of my hope. She would've bugged me until I couldn't even think about Blake.

I know it's true, and it makes my heart hurt. Stacey protected me. I protected her. We had plans. At college we'd meet people who didn't care about brand names and bad music. It all seemed pretty real, when Stacey was alive. Except now she's dead, and there's no magic to make the ache leave.

I slam my locker shut and go home.

Later on I start to feel trapped in my house. I make the mistake of killing time by cleaning my room, and I find an old stack of notes from Stacey. We used to write them in seventh grade. I should put them back where I found them. Instead I look through them. I read them. *Really* read them. And I remember things. Her pet rock named Blinky, the time she broke her arm. And I cry. I cry so hard that I can't see. The only good thing about it is that I realize I might be able to *run* off the emotion. I almost need to.

So ten minutes later I'm doing it. Hitting the pavement, enjoying the ache in my legs. Letting my mind clear.

The relief doesn't last long. Only until I take a wrong turn. By itself, that doesn't matter. What *does* matter is that it's a dead end. A cul-de-sac of houses. And in the middle of it...

It's Blake. Dark hair, messy and perfect at the same time. Hands stuffed into the pockets of his army-green pants. Looking right at me.

Chapter Nine

My feet catch together, and I almost fall. If I wasn't so out of breath, I would've groaned.

You barely see Blake all week, and then you trip in front of him? Nice, Sienna.

He takes a step toward me, and I realize I don't *want* to see him now. I don't want to talk to him. He had all week to come up to me. At lunchtime he pretended I didn't exist. And I'm pissed off.

I spin around, but I'm not quick enough. The moment I face the other way, I hear Blake's voice.

"Sienna?" he calls.

I pump my legs harder and hope he won't follow. No such luck. His voice carries out again. It's louder this time.

"Sienna!" he says.

I pretend not to hear him. I keep going. Quickly I decide not to run in a straight line. That'd make it too easy for Blake. I zigzag instead. I run between houses. Through a couple of backyards. Past some little kid playing hopscotch and then past a couple of barking dogs. I jump over a knee-high fence like some wannabe Olympic star. And I don't stop.

I've definitely gone over my usual half mile. In fact, I'd say this qualifies as some extreme cardio. Which might be the only reason I don't collapse. My body is too full of adrenaline to hurt.

Finally, when I'm pretty sure I can't hear Blake, I slow down. I jog for a few more minutes to be safe. Then I walk. And stop.

"Shit," I say.

I'm on a street I don't recognize. I look around. I actually have no clue where I am.

"Shit," I say again.

Goddamn Blake and his goddamn hair.

It takes me more than an hour to get home. I'm a sweaty, limping mess when I get there. And I'm mad. At Blake. At myself. At Stacey, for sending the triathlon package.

To make things worse, after my shower I get a text message. It's a group thing from some app I don't even use. And it's clearly not meant for me. It's an invite to a party at some guy's house. Chad. I'm pretty sure he's a football player who got suspended for sending out dick pics.

I toss the phone aside. I join my dad in the

living room, where he's watching a game show. But as the minutes tick by, I don't get any less pissed off. I start to regret not confronting Blake.

How dare he keep showing up, then pretend I don't exist? Why did he even bother?

"Asshole," I say, forgetting my dad is in earshot.

"You okay, Sienna?" he asks.

"Fine," I lie.

But I also jump up.

"I'm going to a party," I say.

"That's a new one," he replies.

"I won't be late," I tell him. "I just want to talk to Blake for a minute."

He studies my face for a second, then nods. "You need a ride or any help, let me know."

I quickly get changed. I slap on enough eye makeup to stop a train. I load up my arms with my bracelets and put on my favorite studded necklace. Once I'm ready, I grab the party address from my phone. It's not too far, so I decide to walk.

It's not like I haven't walked even farther today.

I get there pretty quickly, and right away, I'm sorry I came. The place is packed. Jocks galore. Drunk already. I can see at least ten people I'll have to avoid. I almost turn around and go home. But a giggling girl comes up to me and puts her hands on my shoulders.

"I'm *so* glad to see you, Sierra," she says.

I don't bother to correct her on my name. I don't even know hers. And I have no idea why she's glad to see me either.

"Are you thirsty?" she asks. "Do you want a beer?"

I start to shake my head but stop. *There's Blake.* Even from across the room, his perfect hair is unmistakable.

Liquid courage, Sienna?

But I don't drink. I'm allergic to alcohol in a way that makes one sip seem like ten. Stacey and I found that out the hard way.

"Is there any water?" I ask the girl whose name I don't know.

"Uh…there's soda," she replies.

"Sure, okay," I say.

She disappears for a few seconds. I keep my eyes on Blake. He's smiling. Listening to some guy tell a story.

Jerk, I think.

The girl reappears with a plastic cup, full to the brim. I take it from her with a muttered thanks, then lift it to my mouth. I take a small swig. The moment the liquid hits my mouth, I know something's wrong. I spit it out in a spray that makes the girl squeal.

"What the hell is in here?" I ask.

"Vodka, soda, just like you said," she replies.

"That's not what I—" I cut myself off.

There's no point in arguing. The damage is done. The only worry is whether any vodka managed to get into my body.

Dammit, dammit, dammit.

I have to leave. Fast. Before any hint of alcohol hits me and makes me do or say something I'll regret.

Too late, says a gleeful voice in my head.

Blake has spotted me. His smile freezes. He takes a step.

I shove the cup back at the girl. She says something, but I don't hear what it is. I'm already turning. Running away from Blake for the second time today.

Chapter Ten

My second attempt to escape from Blake doesn't go as smoothly as my first. I make it outside and across the lawn. I make it halfway up the block. But this time, there's no shortcut for me to take. I don't have as much of a head start either. In seconds, Blake catches up.

"Hey!" he says. "What the hell's going on?"

I keep walking as I answer. "You tell me."

"What's that supposed to mean?" he replies. "Why are you running away from me?"

"Seriously?" I say.

Blake touches my elbow, but I jerk away.

"Can you stop for a second?" he asks.

"Why would I stop?" I reply.

"Because I want to talk to you?"

"*Right.*" I put a lot of sarcasm into the word. "Just like you wanted to talk to me at school today when all those people were around."

"You wanted me to talk to you at school?" He sounds so surprised that I *do* stop now.

I fix a glare in his direction. "Are you *really* going to pretend you didn't see me today?"

"No," he says. "I saw you. A few times."

I wasn't expecting him to admit it, so I blink at him. "You did?"

He nods. "Yeah. I was at the office during second period. You came in to get a photocopy. And I saw you twice at lunch. First at your locker, then at that big tree outside. Oh. And when I was talking to Bob and those other guys too."

I blink some more. Maybe more vodka got into me than I thought.

"I don't get it," I say.

He shrugs. "I didn't say anything when I saw you because I figured…"

"You figured what?" I ask.

"That you wouldn't want to be seen talking to me," he says.

Now I really think I must be mishearing him. If he said that *he* was embarrassed to be seen with *me*, it would make sense. But this doesn't.

"Why?" I ask.

He runs his hand over his hair. "I dunno. I might bring down your street cred?"

My mouth drops open. And then I laugh. And laugh some more. So hard that my face hurts. I can't help it. When I finally get myself under control, Blake is staring at me.

"Are you drunk?" he asks.

I wave off the question. "It doesn't matter. Did you just say 'street cred'?"

"It *does* matter," he replies. "And yeah. So what?"

"I *want* to think that you're kidding," I say. "But I can tell from your face you aren't. Street cred? Really?"

"What would you call it then?" he asks.

"Call *what*?"

He steps back and looks at me from my head to my toes. I look too. I'm dressed in my standard black. Ripped jeans. Wide belt. Mesh shirt under a baggy tee.

"It's kind of...I don't know." Blake shrugs again. "Unapproachable?"

I start to deny it. But before I can speak, a woman appears at the door of the house where we've stopped.

"Can I help you kids with something?" she asks.

Her tone tells me she hates teenagers. It makes me feel like yelling something back. Possibly about robbing the neighborhood. But Blake is too quick. He calls out to the woman, his voice full of respect.

"No, ma'am," he says. "We were just leaving."

I roll my eyes, but not so the woman can see. When Blake starts walking, I move with him. What he said a second earlier still bugs me. But I wait until we've reached the end of the street before I bring it up.

"So," I say. "That's what you think of me? I'm unapproachable?"

"I don't know if it's what *I* think of you," Blake replies.

"But other people…"

"Yeah. I mean…no offense."

"Okay, fine," I say with a sigh. "So what is it that makes me so scary? Just the clothes? Should I go for a makeover?"

He flashes a grin. "I dunno if a makeover would do it. And there's the whole serial-killer vibe coming from your dad."

"You said my dad was *nice*," I remind him.

"I know. But isn't that what they say about serial killers?" he replies. "Besides, it made you smile."

I almost lift my hand to check if Blake's right. But I can feel the way my mouth is curved up without actually touching it.

"It's a nice smile," he adds.

Blake does that thing where he nudges my shoulder with his, then he slides his hand to mine. The touch makes my tongue stop working.

I'm holding hands with Blake Romano.

Suddenly I wish I could tell Stacey. Badly. It almost ruins the nice tingle that runs up my arm.

Blake clears his throat. "For the record, I don't think you need a makeover."

Heat creeps up my throat. "Thanks."

"No thanks needed," he says. "It's just the truth."

His hand gives mine a squeeze. And now I wish I could tell *him* that I wish I could tell Stacey.

Don't do it, warns a voice in my head.

And I listen to it, thank God.

"Why didn't you run with me this week?" I ask instead.

"Did you want me to?" Blake replies.

"Maybe."

"Say yes, and if you mean it, I'll tell you the truth," he says.

I shake my head. "No way. Not unless you promise to tell me *tonight*."

"I promise to tell you tonight," he says right away.

I roll my eyes. "Yes, I wanted to run with you this week."

Blake smiles, but then he's quiet for a long minute. Was his promise a lie? But finally, keeping his eyes straight ahead, he speaks.

"I was away," he says. "We go away every year for the same few days."

Something about the way he says it makes me frown. Like he worded it too carefully.

"Can we stop for a second?" he asks.

"Sure," I reply.

He lets go of my hand and studies my face. "Would you tell me if you were drunk?"

"Yes," I say. "Why wouldn't I?"

"So you're sober?" he asks.

"Completely," I tell him.

"I'm not sure I should—" Blake cuts himself off. "You know what? Fuck it."

"Fuck what?"

In reply, he leans in. "Tell me if this isn't okay."

And then his lips land on mine.

Chapter Eleven

Blake's mouth is just as soft and warm as I imagined. For a heartbeat, I don't move. Our eyes are locked in a way that might be funny. Then Blake's hand comes up to my cheek, and my eyes close. He kisses me a little harder. I can feel it in every pore. My pulse gets fast, and the world disappears. Finally he pulls away, but only a little.

"Holy shit." I say it under my breath without meaning to.

Blake laughs, and the noise rumbles against my lips. "Thanks. I think."

"You're welcome," I reply.

"I'm sorry for not saying hi at school," he says.

"I was worried you were afraid of being seen with me," I admit.

As soon as the words are out, I regret them. Mostly because they're true. *Too* true.

"I'm not embarrassed to be seen with you, Sienna," Blake says, his tone intense.

I exhale. "Okay."

"I mean it," he says. "And I promise you won't be able to *not* see me at school anymore. If that's what you want."

It's my turn to laugh. "I'll think about it and get back to you."

He brushes my lips in another quick kiss, then

lets me go. "Your house is around the corner. Can I walk you to the gate?"

I nod. "Sure."

"Do you want to run tomorrow?" he asks. "Or bike?"

"Maybe on Sunday?" I reply.

For the next minute of walking, I hope he'll grab my hand again, but he doesn't. In fact, he's really quiet. He barely says goodbye before he leaves. Does it mean he regrets kissing me? My heart beats faster again. Only now it's *not* a good thing. It's not until I'm halfway to the door that I hear his voice again.

"Hey, Sienna?" he calls.

I turn around. "Yeah?"

"Remind me on Sunday to tell you why my family and I go away this week every year, okay?" he says.

I nod, and he slips away. Like always, I watch him go.

Why is he always so damn mysterious? I wonder.

But I forget about it quickly. My brain is stuck on the kiss.

Avoiding my dad, I sneak up to my room. I get ready for bed, replaying the kiss in my head.

I don't know if I'll be able to sleep at all, but I'm wrong. The moment I pull up my blanket, I drift off. And the next thing I know, the sun is shining through my window.

I make sure to keep busy all day Saturday. I help my dad with stuff he's been begging me to do for months. I weed the garden. Fix a shelf. Dig out an old cookbook and make a casserole. I do my best not to think about Blake. Or about his lips. Weirdly, I'm tempted to run, but I don't do it.

Gotta save it for Sunday, Sienna, I tell myself.

I stay up later than I should. Especially considering how early I have to get up. But I want to be so tired that I collapse. And it works. Almost. When I crawl into bed that night, my eyes are heavy. My pillow has never been more comfortable. Except just as I'm falling asleep, a noise yanks me awake again.

Tick-tick.

My heart speeds up.

The sound comes again.

Tick-tick.

I tug my blankets tighter.

Tick-tick.

Is it coming from my window?

Slowly I roll to face it.

Tick-tick.

I open my eyes a tiny bit. Just in time to see something—two somethings—hit the glass.

Tick-tick.

"What the hell?" I mutter.

I push my blanket off, stand up and walk toward the window. I stand a bit back from it and peek outside. It's Blake. He's standing in the yard. As I watch, he throws two tiny rocks.

Tick-tick.

I look over my shoulder to make sure my door is closed, then step into view. Blake waves.

"Seriously?" I say even though he can't hear me.

He waves again, and I slide open the window.

"What the hell are you doing?" I ask.

"It's an emergency," he replies. "Can I come up?"

"Does it *look* like there's a way to come up?"

"Then can you come down?"

"Fine," I say. "Wait there. And don't make any more noise."

Being extra quiet, I sneak down the stairs. I don't breathe until I'm outside and standing across from Blake. I grab his arm and tug him away from the house. I pull him to a bench beside our garage and push him down. I have no idea what my dad would do if he caught me. But I don't want to find out.

"What do you want?" I ask in a whisper.

"I can't make it tomorrow morning," Blake says, almost as quietly. "One of my sisters is sick, and

I have to babysit again."

"You couldn't send a text?" I reply.

"I don't have your number," he says.

"Oh. Right." I pause. "Well, we can go on a different day, can't we?"

Blake inclines his head, then looks away. In his lap, his hands close into fists.

"She died," he says.

For a second I think he's talking about Stacey. But he quickly speaks again, and I realize he's talking about his mom.

"When I said she's been gone for five years," he says, "what I really meant was that she killed herself five years ago."

My heart drops and aches at the same time. "I'm sorry."

How many times has someone said that to me in the last five months? I never really understood it. Not until this second. I *am* sorry. Sorry for what he lost. Sorry for not being able to fix it. Sorry for every drop of sadness. But the words aren't quite enough. Because words aren't ever enough. I reach over and take his hand. He threads his fingers through mine.

"I'm sorry too," Blake says. "I wanted you to know because I think you might understand."

My throat is scratchy. I don't understand what it's like to lose a parent like that. But I get what it's like to lose someone you love more than life. And it makes a little more sense why he wanted to talk to me in the first place.

"Every year, on the anniversary of her death, we take a trip," he says. "We go somewhere different each time, but we always go. My dad calls it 'honoring Mom.' I think he's just trying to get away from it, you know?"

I nod. "Yeah, I get it."

His thumb traces a small circle on the back of

my hand. "Thanks for not just telling me to fuck off when I came up to you in the caf."

Any other time, the statement would've made me laugh. Or maybe roll my eyes. But I just nod again, and I lean in to put my head on Blake's shoulder. We stay that way for at least five minutes before he sighs.

"I should go," he says. "My dad will freak if he walks by my room and sees I'm not there."

"Mine too," I reply.

But what I'm really thinking is that I don't want this moment to end. For the first time since Stacey died, I feel like someone really sees me.

Chapter Twelve

I run alone on Sunday. I do the same on Monday. I bike on Tuesday, but on Wednesday I let myself rest. Blake doesn't come to school on any of those days. I'm sure of it, because I overhear Alec the douche talking about it to some other guy.

I ask myself the same question about a thousand times. *Why didn't I give him my number?* At least then we would've been able to talk or text. I do try to stalk him a bit, but Blake's got his social media locked down. And despite the kiss and everything else, I'm too chickenshit to click *follow*.

It's weird to miss him. It's even weirder to not think about Stacey quite so much. It makes me feel guilty. Except when I'm running. Then everything kind of falls away.

On Thursday I decide to run after school. I'm trying a different route. Something longer. I don't even set my watch to track it. I just go and go. The burn in my legs is good now. The sweat makes me proud. I'm not fast. A lady with a jogging stroller passes me at one point. But I'm okay with it. Two weeks ago I wouldn't have been able to do this at all.

I keep going until I realize where I've taken myself. The trail that leads to Lively Lake.

I slow down, then walk.

So much for not thinking about Stacey.

I could turn around. I know if I keep going, my heart is going to hurt even more. But something makes me push through it.

Drawing a deep breath, I make my way into the woods. For a while I stay on the main path. But after a couple of minutes, I spot the marker I've been looking for. A green ribbon stapled to a stump. There, I cut into the trees. Right away the forest gets thicker, blocking out the sun. The body heat from my run fades. I wrap my arms around my body and ignore both the cold and the prick of branches on my skin.

A few more minutes, and I reach an opening in the woods. In front of me is a spot I know well. A swimming hole. It looks like a picture. The water is still and clear. Tiny rocks and sand line the edges.

In my head, I see Stacey standing there. Arms over her head. Diving in with a laugh.

She loved this place. She never cared how cold

it was. She was always ready to swim. Sometimes she'd jump in with her clothes on.

"I miss you," I say out loud. "Why did you have to leave?"

There's no answer. Just a breeze that ruffles my hair.

I think about the triathlon. About Stacey gleefully signing us up. All the running and biking I've been doing. I think about the joke I made to Blake about not bringing me a swimsuit. Except now I wish he was here.

Should I swim?

I glance back and forth. It's way too cold out for anyone else to be here now. Even in the summer, most of the kids like a different swimming spot anyway.

Just go for it, Sienna. What've you got to lose?

"Right," I say. "Just my pride."

I take another quick look around, then walk to the edge of the water. I kick out of my shoes and socks and rip off my shirt. I peel down my jogging pants. For a moment I stand there in my sports bra and underwear. My skin is covered in goose bumps.

Now or never. And it's gotta be now.

With a big inhale, I run forward into the water. It splashes up, icy on my legs.

"Shit, shit, shit!" I gasp.

But I don't let myself stop. I lift up my arms and dive right in.

Icy water sucks around my body. It steals my breath. But I still don't give up. I paddle into the deepest part of the swimming hole, and then I really swim. I'm sure it's not awesome. I can hardly remember how to do a front crawl. But my arms move. My feet kick. I work just as hard as if I were running or biking. I'm feeling pretty damn good about it. Again I wish Blake was here. He'd love this.

We could swim. Talk. *Kiss.*

Then I hear a laugh.

I freeze so suddenly that I go under. Water slides up my nose, and I burst back up, coughing. My eyes go to the shore.

Alec goddamn Tater Tot.

He's standing there with three guys and two girls. He's watching me. There's a shit-eating grin on his face. I know what he's planning before he even does it. But my voice refuses to work.

"See you later, fatty!" he yells.

A heartbeat later, he grabs my clothes and runs off with them. His friends follow. I'm left in the water, wearing next to nothing.

Chapter Thirteen

For two minutes I tread water. My breaths get shorter. My legs hurt more than when I run. I can't stay where I am, but I'm scared to swim to shore. I'm even scared to roll onto my back and float. I don't want to take my eyes off the trees.

Are they waiting for me? Are they up there in the forest? What is Alec planning?

If I'm lucky, he just wanted to take my clothes. If I'm not, he could have the camera on his phone ready or something.

"Asshole," I say.

Another minute or more passes.

I have to give in.

Heart thumping, I swim slowly toward the shore. I stop when my feet can touch the bottom. I stand there for a while too. There's no sign of the jerks who took my stuff. And they don't seem like the patient type.

Now I'm shivering. I can't wait any longer.

Crouched low, I move forward, inch by inch. When I have to, I drop to my knees. I crawl. The rocks under me bite into my skin. The whole time, I don't take my stare away from the trees.

There's no one there, I tell myself over and over.

And if they *are,* then a video of my escape is going to be more embarrassing than a picture anyway.

I reach the shore and stand up. Wildly I look around, and I see that I'm not alone after all. A girl is sitting on a rock nearby, watching me in silence.

My face burns. But I'm mad. So pissed off that I don't even try to cover myself up. I put my hands on my hips and glare.

"What the hell do you want?" I ask.

The girl looks unsure, but she answers me. "I've got your clothes. And your phone's here too."

"Yeah, right," I say.

She holds up a pile of fabric. It *is* my stuff. But I still don't trust her.

"I can just leave it here," she says. "I get it if you don't want to talk to me. But I wanted to tell you I told Alec and them to fuck off."

She sounds like she means it, and I'm surprised to almost believe her.

"You did?" I reply.

She nods. "And if you want someone to walk home with…"

I study her for a few seconds. If she wanted to do something shitty to me, she's had plenty of time. And I'm already practically naked.

"Fine," I say, "but if I find out that Alec and those other assholes are hiding somewhere…"

"They're not," she replies. "I swear."

I hurry the rest of the way out of the water. I take my clothes from her quickly. And I don't bother trying to dry off before I get dressed. But Alec doesn't pop out from the woods. There's no muffled laughter.

Maybe she does *mean it.*

"You don't know who I am, do you?" she asks once I'm fully clothed.

There's no point in lying, so I shake my head. "No idea."

"Marsha Johnson," she says. "We were in kindergarten together. You came to my sixth birthday party."

I frown. A vague memory comes to mind. But I can't place it, so I shrug.

"Sorry," I say.

"It's okay," she replies. "I turned six right before—"

Marsha cuts herself off, but I suddenly remember. Her party had been at a gymnastics place. It was a Sunday. And the next day was Stacey's first day at our school. We became instant best friends. Weird guilt hits me. Would I have become friends with Marsha if I hadn't met Stacey?

No, I think. *I wouldn't be friends with someone who hangs out with Alec. Not in a gazillion years.*

"I'm sorry those assholes took your stuff," Marsha says.

Again, she sounds like she means it.

"Why are you friends with them?" I ask.

Together we start walking away from the swimming hole.

"I'm not really," Marsha tells me. "My friend Cal

likes his friend Aidan, so we always just wind up, you know, hanging out. Sucks. But Cal's my friend, so…you know what that's like." She rolls her eyes. "Oh, hey, can I ask you something?"

The question makes me tense. I brace for her to wonder some terrible thing about Stacey. But she doesn't.

"Do you have Ming for pre-calc?" she asks instead. "Because I do, and that homework she gave out is killer. I thought my brain was going to explode."

For the next few minutes, Marsha talks about how much she hates math. Then how much she loves art. She tells me the name of her favorite band and asks mine. I answer her questions until it feels almost normal to be doing it. And suddenly we're on the road back into town.

"I've gotta go this way," she says, pointing. "Cal's expecting me to show up again. But it was awesome talking to you."

"Thanks for getting my clothes," I reply.

"Yeah, no problem. Sorry again about those douches." She pauses. "You want to eat lunch with me and Cal next week sometime?"

The question startles me. "Uh. Maybe."

"Alec won't be there, I promise."

"That's a big selling point," I say.

She laughs. "See you."

I wave, but when she turns away, I call her name. "Marsha?"

She looks back. "Yeah?"

"It was good talking to you too," I say.

She shrugs. "Would've talked to you anytime you wanted."

Then she takes off for real. Just like I've done with Blake, I watch her go. A weird feeling is in my chest. I can't quite explain it. I'm sad. And guilty. It was always Stacey and me against the world. But what Marsha just said makes me second-guess that.

And I don't want *to second-guess it.*

I don't want to wonder if Stacey and I held each other back. More important, I don't want to wonder if *she* held *me* back.

My stomach hurts, and tears prick my eyes.

I'm suddenly mad at Marsha. How dare she be nice to me? How dare she tell Alec off and help me?

Like a little kid, I pick up a rock and chuck it as far as I can. It bounces into the road just as a car comes around the corner. I hold my breath, eyes wide. At the last second, the rock bounces again, saving the car. Saving me from about a year of being grounded.

My shoulders sag. It's not Marsha's fault. And I don't wish things had been different with Stacey. I just wish she was alive. I wish she'd talked to me more about her feelings. I knew she was hurting. I just didn't know how badly. And I wish someone could understand this ache.

Blake does. Blake understands.

And the need to see him overtakes me.

Chapter Fourteen

Finding Blake's house is easy enough. I type his last name into an online directory, and a nearby address pops up. It even has an option to get directions. I click that. And in ten minutes I'm standing in front of his house.

Am I really doing this?

I bite my lip. Two weeks ago I would've crossed

the street to avoid Blake. If I saw him at school, I would've looked down and pretended not to.

That's all different now.

Or I hope it is anyway.

My feet don't move fast. But even before I get to the front porch, the door opens. It's not Blake who's standing there, though. It's a man who looks exactly like him but older. He greets me with a grin that's just like Blake's too.

"Hey!" he says. "You must be Blake's girlfriend. Sienna, right?"

My face gets very hot, very fast. "I'm not—"

Blake steps out, cutting me off. "Hi, Sienna. Is everything okay?"

I nod.

"Invite her in," his dad says.

"I'm going to, Dad," Blake replies. "Jeez."

They both step aside so that I can come in.

No going back now.

Pushing down my nerves, I move into the entry-way. Blake grabs my hand and tugs me down the hall to his bedroom.

"Door open, bud!" his dad calls.

Blake makes a face but yells, "Yeah, I know!"

I shift from foot to foot. Now that I'm standing here in front of him—in his space—I don't know what to say. My worries about Marsha and Stacey and *life* seem to have disappeared. Blake's room distracts me. His walls are covered in rock-band posters. Unsurprisingly, he has a shelf full of sports trophies. The whole place smells exactly like him. It's like being hit with a Blake-themed truck.

After a second he clears his throat and says, "Your hair is wet."

"I went swimming," I reply.

The rest of the story follows. My run. My swim. Marsha. My thoughts about Stacey and me. When I'm done, some weight lifts off my shoulders. But Blake is quiet.

"Aren't you going to say anything?" I ask.

"All I'm hearing is that I missed a chance to see you in your underwear," he replies.

Of course, I blush. "Perv."

He grins and nudges my shoulder. He's too damn cute for his own good.

"I wish I'd been there," he says. "And not just because of the underwear. I'd love to swim with you. And I'd have kicked Alec's ass."

I laugh. The weight gets even lighter. I'm glad I came. I open my mouth to admit it to Blake, but he stops me with a kiss. His mouth is even warmer than I remember. And this time, he puts his arms around my waist and tucks his hands against my lower back.

I'm melting.

My whole body is warm. I'm pressed right against Blake, so close that I can feel his skin through his shirt. The sandalwood smell fills my nose even more. It fills my *pores.* Like it's a part of me. I don't want this to end. So when Blake's dad yells from somewhere in the house, I resent it.

Blake laughs against my lips. "Sorry. One of my sisters probably needs something. Can you wait here for a minute?"

"No," I say.

He pulls back, his eyes wide with surprise. "Really?"

I give Blake's chest a push. "No, not *really*. I'll be here when you get back."

"Promise?"

"Yes."

He kisses my forehead, then my nose, then my mouth. "See you in a sec."

He leaves me standing in the middle of the room with my heart beating hard. I press my hand to my chest. It's a good feeling. I take a minute to enjoy it. But when Blake doesn't come back right away, I start to look around.

I study his trophies. There's one for every sport a person could think of. There's also one from a fourth-grade spelling bee. I read the names on the band posters. Blake seems to like classic rock more than my dad does.

I flick a look to his bed. It's made. Gray sheets and a black blanket. I touch the pillow and blush as I imagine him lying there. I start to turn away, but a notebook on the nightstand catches my eye. It's purple. And familiar in a way that makes my hands close up. But it can't be what I think it is.

Stacey's journal.

Heart racing, I pick it up. I flip it open. There, on the pages, my best friend's handwriting stands out. I don't see the words. My eyes are too blurred by tears.

"Sienna?" says Blake.

I lift my head. He's standing in the doorway.

"What the hell is this?" I ask, holding out the journal.

"It's not what you think," he replies.

He tries to reach for the book, but I jerk it back.

"It's not my dead best friend's diary?" I ask.

"It is, but let me explain," Blake says.

"Not a chance in hell," I tell him. "There's nothing you can say that will make this okay."

I hear him calling after me, but I ignore him. I tear through the house and burst out the door. I don't stop running until I'm all the way home. I collapse on the grass in front of my house. The journal is in my hands. I'm holding it so tightly that it hurts. My brain and heart hurt too.

Blake Romano, jock. Blake Romano, best kisser in the world. Blake Romano, liar and thief.

No wonder it felt like I knew him. He'd read my best friend's most private thoughts. He'd used them to get to me. What was his plan? Get me to have sex with him? Make me think he loved me?

I cry even harder. I haven't cried this hard since Stacey's funeral.

Betrayal is everywhere. And it's time to put a wall back up around my heart.

Chapter Fifteen

For the next three days, I pretend to be sick. It's not hard, actually. My stomach does ache. I keep crying, so I look like shit. My dad doesn't even question it.

What about your running? a little voice in my head asks.

But I push it away. The race is coming up fast. The weekend after next. If I'm going to do it, I need to keep training.

"Three days off won't kill me," I whisper to myself.

Avoiding Blake is more important anyway. He got my number somehow. He's texted me a hundred times. Called so much that I blocked his number.

I'm fully planning on staying home for a fourth day too. Maybe even a fifth. But my dad starts talking about seeing the doctor. So I drag my ass out of bed. I go for a run. And I go to school. It's easy enough to stay away from Blake. I managed to do it for a long time before this. Every time I even *think* I see him, I want to run the other way.

I eat lunch with Marsha. Her friend Cal seems nice, even if she has bad taste in guys.

I'm less alone than I've been in ages. But I've never felt so lonely.

I bike. I run. I hang out with my dad.

I don't touch Stacey's diary. I don't want to read it. It doesn't seem right. By Friday I still haven't touched it. But later that night my dad knocks on my bedroom door.

"Come in!" I call.

He has an envelope in his hands. "This came for you."

Right away I'm nervous. The last envelope that came was the triathlon package. A message from the grave.

"Thanks, Dad," I make myself say.

"You okay, kiddo?" he asks.

"Little tired," I reply. "Too much homework."

He hesitates. "You know you can talk to me about anything, right?"

"I know, Dad," I say.

He leaves, closing the door behind him.

I study the envelope. It has my name and address on it. Nothing about Stacey, thank God. But there's no postage on it. No return address.

With sweaty palms, I tear it open. And a note falls out and lands in my lap. It's written in block letters.

I DIDN'T STEAL IT. I SWEAR. I FOUND IT A MONTH AGO, AND I OPENED IT WITHOUT KNOWING. STACEY LOVED YOU. SHE MADE ME WANT TO KNOW YOU. I THINK YOU SHOULD SEE YOURSELF THROUGH HER EYES. READ IT. PLEASE. IF YOU STILL HATE ME AFTER, I'LL LEAVE YOU ALONE FOREVER. BUT JUST IN CASE, I'LL BE WAITING FOR YOU AT THE FINISH LINE. —BLAKE

For a minute I'm mad all over again. But after a few seconds, I calm down. I reread his note. I look over at the diary on my shelf and bite my lip.

Will a few pages hurt?

"Probably," I say.

But only because it *all* hurts.

I grab it and flip open the first page. The first thing I see is my own name.

Sienna made me laugh until I cried today. I don't know what I'd do without her.

Slowly, with more tears flowing, I read a little more.

Stacey wrote down a lot of things. Stories about her day. About *our* day. Good things. Bad things. So much sadness. There were poems. There was rage. A frustration over why she couldn't climb out of the blackness of her mind. She was hurting. All the time. But I could see—really see—that I had mattered to her.

It takes me the whole weekend to read it all. When I'm done, I feel like I've lost my best friend all over again. My grief is fresh. So is my anger that she left. But at the same time, it's like I get a piece of her back. And Blake is right. I like who I was in Stacey's mind. I like how she saw me.

I'm still not any less pissed off that Blake read the diary. It wasn't meant for him. But I'm glad it was Stacey who led him to me. And I get it. I get why, after losing his mom the same way, he'd want to read it.

I spend the next week thinking about Stacey's words. And I keep training for the triathlon. I run.

I bike. I even go to the pool twice, shoving down my embarrassment about being in a bathing suit in public.

I keep avoiding Blake. I'm just not ready to face him yet.

Then Saturday comes, and it's time for the race. I pack my stuff and head down. It starts at Lively Lake. Something I didn't realize until that morning. It seems to fit, though, and I like it.

When I get there, the place is crowded. I'm more self-conscious by the second. My shorts are too tight. My legs are too thick. The extra roll on my stomach is too obvious. Because even though I've been training for weeks, I'm not suddenly a fitness pro. I'm still *me*. The "try hard."

Am I really cut out for this?

But pretty soon it's too busy around me to think about anything. And it's obvious that I'm not the only one doing this for the first time. There are kids and grandparents. Some random little girl even grabs my hand and tells me she likes my hair. I'd put a purple streak in it the night before.

Before I can believe it, I'm standing with my group. When the starter gun goes off, we all surge into the water.

In my head, I hear Stacey's voice. *Go, go, go!*

I swim hard. I almost laugh at how quickly the first part is done. I barely have time to work up to a front crawl, and then I'm climbing out. Running for the transition area where my bike is waiting.

I towel off. Toss on a shirt. And I'm off again.

I get a wave from the same little girl who said she liked my hair. She's on a green bike, and she dings her bell at me and grins. I ride along beside her, smiling back.

The bike course is quick too. My forehead is only just starting to bead with sweat when I finish it.

At last it's time to run.

I burst onto the marked path, going at full speed.

By now I've realized that this race is designed to be easy. To make people want to do it.

I don't hold back. And it's not Stacey's voice I hear in my head anymore. It's Blake's.

Go, go, go!

But very quickly I realize his voice isn't in my head. It's right there for real. *Blake* is there for real. I see him at the finish line, just like he promised.

"Go, Sienna!" he yells. "You've got this."

I run even harder. Even faster. I swear that I'm the first person in my group to cross the line. And I run straight to Blake. I throw myself into his arms like someone who just ran an actual marathon. I'm sweaty, but I don't even care. His sandalwood smell feels like coming home. Like a beginning.

I might still be Sienna Shoring, the girl with the dead best friend. But I'm also Sienna Shoring, the girl with a life worth living.

Star Spider

HEY JUDE

Penny is busy enough with school and taking care of her sister. She doesn't have time for love, but then she meets Jack.

⭐ "An emotionally layered book."
—*Kirkus Reviews*, starred review

When his father is killed under mysterious circumstances, Will returns home and begins to fall for the girl he never thought he would see again.

"A twisty noir mystery."
—*Kirkus Reviews*

MOTEL

SULFUR HEART

BROOKE CARTER

Melinda Di Lorenzo has been writing professionally for more than a decade, and is the author of *Counting Scars* in the Orca Soundings line. In 2013 she won Harlequin's annual *So You Think You Can Write* contest, which came with a publishing contract and launched her successfully into the romance world. Bullied as a teen, Melinda sought refuge in books. She now wants to bring that refuge to others, and she draws on her experience as the parent of three teens to craft stories that reflect modern struggles without turning those struggles into stereotypes. She also supports young writers and makes an annual creative writing scholarship donation to École Salish Secondary. She lives in Vancouver, British Columbia.

orca soundings

For more information on all the books

in the Orca Soundings line, please visit

orcabook.com